Celebrate Diversity

Written and Illustrated by Dee Smith

Copyright © 2016

Visit Deesignery.com

Celebrate diversity. Celebrate you.

Celebrate what makes you different, wonderful and true.

Celebrate kindness. Celebrate friends.

Celebrate the days where any sadness quickly ends.

Celebrate coming together. Celebrate love.

Celebrate conquering frustration and then rising above.

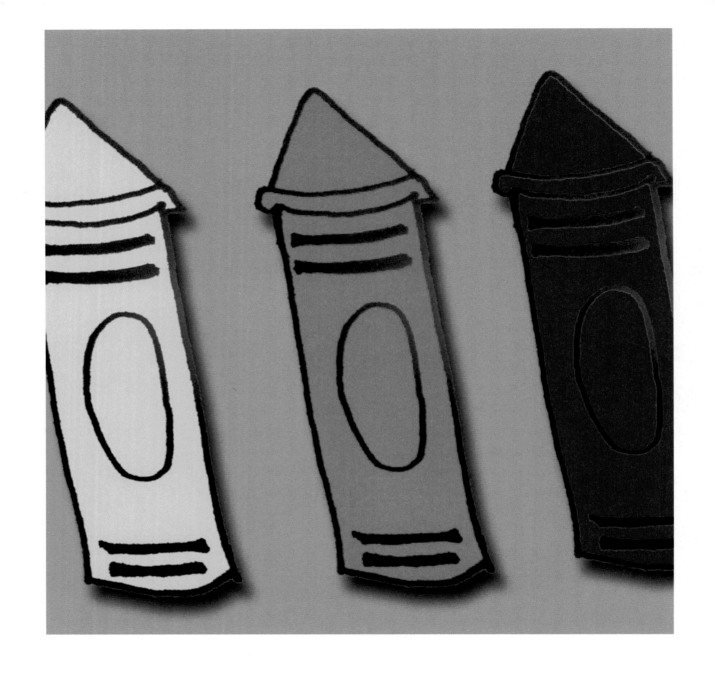

Celebrate difference. Celebrate it now.

Prejudice and intolerance we will not allow.

Celebrate the beautiful things that make us all one of a kind.

Celebrate that beauty, in everyone, is an easy thing to find.

Celebrate my uniqueness. I'll celebrate you.

Let's celebrate diversity. We'll make our dreams come true.

Let's celebrate diversity. Let's celebrate today!

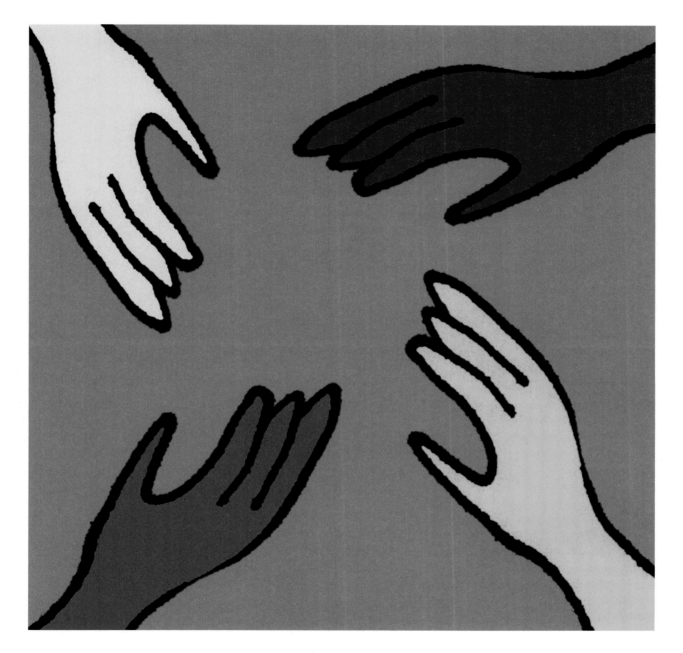

For friendship, love and acceptance
we shall pave the way.

Follow your dreams.

Here are a few fun easy ways you can make a difference on any day

Lend a helping hand

Be a friend

Recycle

Comfort someone when they are feeling down.

Do an act of kindness

This book is dedicated to anyone who has ever felt strange or different.

Always Remember your uniqueness makes you uniquely you!

~Dee

Thank You!

Thank you so much for reading this book.
It means the world to me!
If you liked the book I would much appreciate if you would write a Review on Amazon. I am so thankful for each and every person supporting my dream of being a writer for children. Because you have read this book, yes that means YOU too! Thanks Again!
Stay tuned for more titles on my website Deesignery.com

Regards,
Dee

About the Author:

My name is Dee Smith. I am an Author and Illustrator. My hobbies include graphic design, puppetry, balloon twisting, drawing and of course writing. I am dedicated to my mission of keeping children entertained in fun and innovative ways.

Looking for More books about Diversity and Acceptance?
Read Unique and Wonderful Next!

Unique and Wonderful- A Rhyming picture book for children that encourages tolerance.

See what the Buzz is all about!
Take a journey to Bee-ville

Read this fun series about a small bee that goes on big adventures and learns along the way!

Have you ever felt like dancing in the rain?

Read this rhyming book about a girl who loves to dance when it starts to drizzle.

Made in the USA
Middletown, DE
05 June 2020